THE WHALE
WHO WANTED MORE

For all the souls of this Uni-verse*,
who are remembering the tune. — R B
*(One-song)

For my littlest nephew Charlie
— welcome to the world — J F

ORCHARD BOOKS

First published in Great Britain in 2021
by The Watts Publishing Group

3 5 7 9 10 8 6 4

Text © Rachel Bright, 2021
Illustrations © Jim Field, 2021

The moral rights of the author and illustrator have been asserted.

A CIP catalogue record for this book is available from the British Library.

HB ISBN 978 1 40834 923 6
PB ISBN 978 1 40834 922 9

Printed and bound in Spain

MIX
Paper from
responsible sources
FSC® C104740
FSC
www.fsc.org

Orchard Books, an imprint of Hachette Children's Group
Part of The Watts Publishing Group Limited
Carmelite House,
50 Victoria Embankment,
London EC4Y 0DZ
An Hachette UK Company
www.hachette.co.uk
www.hachettechildrens.co.uk

ORCHARD

Rachel
BRIGHT

Jim
FIELD

THE WHALE
WHO WANTED MORE

Under glittering waves of a vast ocean blue,

A beautiful world is hidden from view.

And there, in the cool and the quiet of the deep,

A great, gentle giant was stirring from sleep.

With a hubbub of bubbles, he opened one eye
And let out a long, lonely, rippling sigh.

For when Humphrey awoke, he remembered his QUEST,

One that pulled at his heart and pressed at his chest.

A life-longing search for . . . he didn't know what . . .

He just KNEW it was something he hadn't yet got!

He'd rifled in shipwrecks and rooted through treasure,

Scooped pretty shells, which
he'd polish for pleasure.

But whether his haul
was enormous or tiny . . .

. . . The next day, it just never seemed quite as **SHINY.**

So he **NEVER** felt satisfied, that was for sure,
And, no matter the bounty, he just wanted **MORE**.

BUT, the more he amassed, the more lonesome he got.
He knew it was wrong, but he just couldn't stop.

So he drifted, without any sense of direction,
Till his WANDERINGS washed him, one day . . .

...TO PERFECTION!

A rainbow of reefs
kissed with speckles of sun,
Where all kinds of critters
hung out and had fun.
There were glistening fishes,
crustaceans galore,
There were molluscs and dugongs
and urchins and more!

The coral was studded with
flotsam and jetsam.
Humphrey just wanted to
dive in and get some!

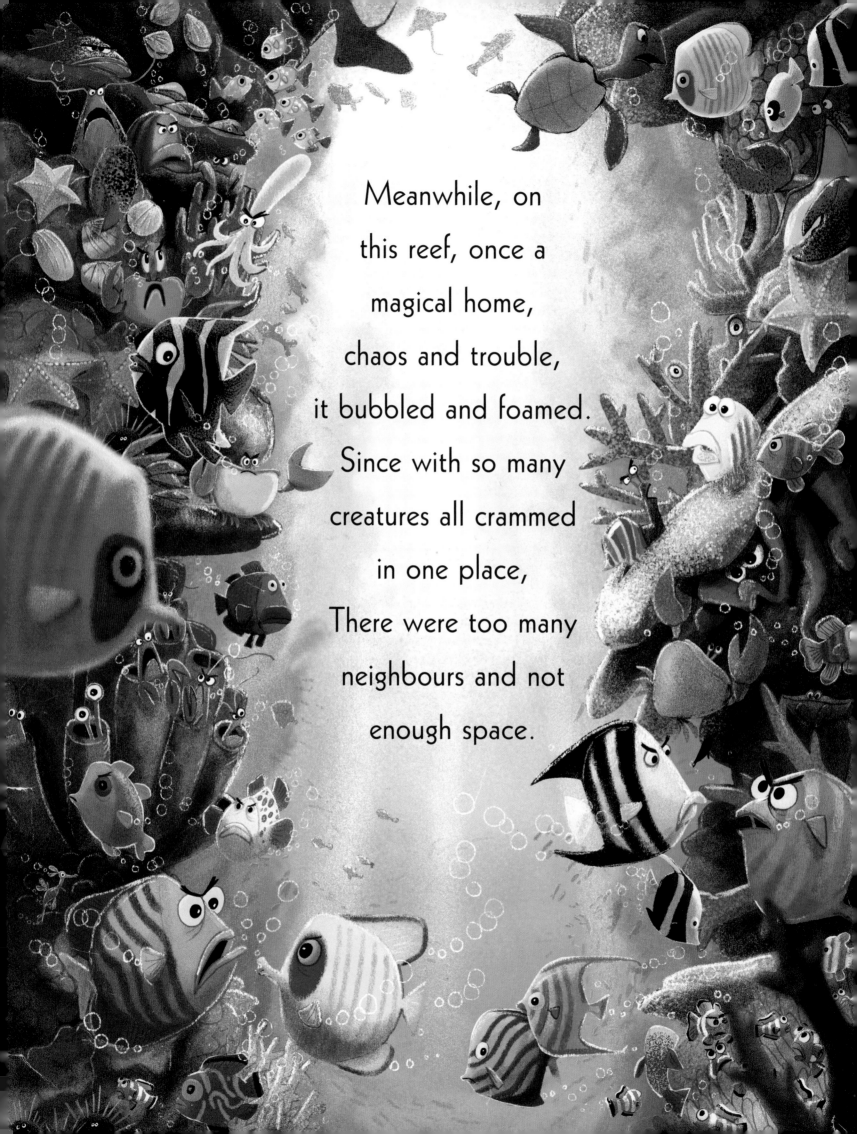

Meanwhile, on
this reef, once a
magical home,
chaos and trouble,
it bubbled and foamed.
Since with so many
creatures all crammed
in one place,
There were too many
neighbours and not
enough space.

They all **BICKERED** and **SNIPPERED**.

 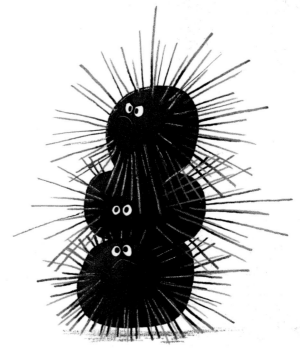

They **PUSHED** and they **SHOVED**.

And so did not notice . . .

. . . the
SHADOW
above.

Except . . . **ONE** with a curious stalk of an eye,
Which luckily always gazed up at the sky!
A crab with quick wit and a brilliant mind,
Crystal was smart and eternally kind.

"**LOOK UP!**" Crystal shouted.
"**LOOK UP AND LOOK OUT,
THE WHALE WHO WANTS MORE
IS OUT AND ABOUT!**"

But all were so busy
with one gripe or another,
They hadn't got time
to look out for each other.
So Humphrey, he plunged
in the noise of the brawl
to fill up his longing

ONCE AND FOR ALL!

"HELLLLLLP!" they all screamed,
gripped by panic and fear.
But, as everyone froze,
Crystal's thinking was clear . . .

"**WHALE!**"
Crystal shouted.
"**WHALE,
YOU
MUST
STOP!**"
She yelled it so loud that
she thought she might pop!
"**YOU** are the Whale who
ALWAYS wants **MORE**,
But **WHAT** are you
really wanting it
FOR?"

Well, Humphrey was
utterly taken aback.
This feisty young crab stopped
him still in his track!

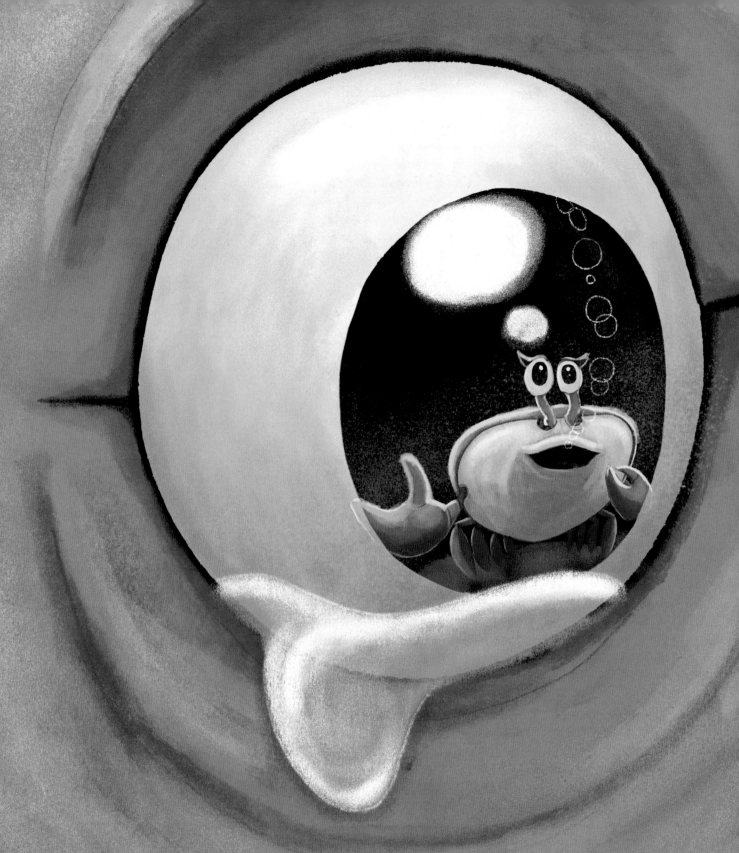

He thought very hard, for the first time in years,
As he gathered his voice, so he fought back some tears.
"I . . . don't . . . know," whispered Humphrey. "I think that my goal
Was to feel all filled-up and, well, happy and . . . WHOLE."

"You know," replied Crystal, "I think you might find
That happiness comes when you're CARING and KIND.
Perhaps . . ." she suggested, with one pincer uncurled,
"You might have a gift you could GIVE to the world?"

Humphrey, he hung on her every word,
And deep in his soul, a melody stirred.
He remembered a lullaby, taught by his mother,
Echoed through time from one whale to another.

"I **WAS** given one gift, when I was brand-new,
But I've never had someone to **GIVE** that gift to . . ."

Then he opened his mouth, let go of his doubt . . .
And an achingly beautiful tune tumbled out.
The turtles, they circled, the dolphins were playing,
Even the seaweed was dancing and swaying!

And as harmony touched
every one who was there,
They remembered that balance
takes patience and care.

They'd been fighting
and poking and
griping so long,
They'd forgotten they
all sang the same

OCEAN SONG.
Humphrey, he knew then,
he wanted to stay,
As at last, all his
longings . . . they had
faded away.

From then, all was rhythm and peace on the reef.

For one clever young crab, it was quite a relief.

She befriended the whale, who perfected the knack

Of taking the time to GIVE some things back.

Yes, that whale stopped collecting
and made a great start
At doing the things that
FILLED UP his heart.

So perhaps true contentment,
is not about STUFF...

. . . Since we all need
SO LITTLE
to have quite enough.